In the beginning, the Spirit of the Earth gave every animal a wooden box with a gift inside. One by one, the animals opened the boxes.

One box contained all of the rivers and lakes. The next contained all of the hills and mountains. Then came all of the trees and seeds. Then came the wind, to carry those seeds far and wide.

Soon all of the boxes were open except one. Gull kept his box shut and locked.

"This is my box. I can do whatever I like with it," he said.

Gull's box contained all of the sunshine. Without the sunshine, the Earth was in darkness all of the time.

All of the animals got tired of stumbling about in the dark. They begged Gull to let out some of the sunshine.

"I cannot see my food," complained Rabbit.

"I cannot see who is sitting next to me," complained Robin.

But the more they begged, the more Gull held onto his box.

“You cannot need all of that sunshine,” said Gull’s friend, Raven.

“It is meant for everyone, not just for you. Give us some of it.”

But Gull shook his head. He planned to keep all of the sunshine for himself.

Raven tried to flatter Gull into letting out some of the sunshine.

“Gull, you are so clever and good-looking. Can you let us see what is inside your box?”

But Gull just shook his head again.

Then Raven got angry and he shouted at Gull.

"You are selfish and horrible!" he yelled.

But Gull still kept his box locked.

Then Raven had a long think, and he hatched a cunning plan. He gathered some prickly thorns and laid them out on the ground by Gull's boat.

Then he called out, “Gull, Gull, come quickly! Your boat is floating off!”

Gull came running out of his tent – straight onto the prickly thorns, which got stuck in his feet.

“Ouch!” he cried.

"Do not panic," said Raven. "I will take out the thorns. Just unlock your box to let out a little sunshine so that I can see them."

Gull opened his box a little bit.

But Raven said, “I still cannot see to get the thorns out.”

So Gull opened the box a bit more.

"I still cannot see the thorns properly," said Raven. "Can you open the box a little wider?"

So Gull took the lid off the box. But when he did so, all of the sunshine escaped!

Raven got the thorns out of his friend's feet. Then he chuckled to himself as Gull tried and failed to get the sunshine back into the box.

From that point on, sunshine lit the Earth.

And Gull stood on one leg, shouting, “Ou, ou, ou!”